For the real Sosha . . . Who else?

I Love You, Mr. Bear
Copyright © 2003 by Sylvie Wickstrom
Manufactured in China by South China Printing Company Ltd. All rights reserved.
www.harperchildrens.com

Library of Congress Cataloging-in-Publication Data
Wickstrom, Sylvie.
I love you, Mister Bear / by Sylvie Wickstrom.—1st ed.
p.   cm.
Summary: Young Sosha buys a shaggy old teddy bear at a yard sale and brings him home for some special care and love.
ISBN 0-06-029331-4 — ISBN 0-06-029332-2 (lib. bdg.)
[1. Teddy bears—Fiction.] I. Title.
PZ7.W6295Ik 2004
[E]—dc21
2003001103

Typography by Matt Adamec
1 2 3 4 5 6 7 8 9 10
❖
First Edition

SYLVIE WICKSTROM

I Love You, Mister Bear

YARD SALE!

HARPERCOLLINS*PUBLISHERS*

Bear for Sale

Look, Daddy. A yard sale.
Let's check it out.

Nothing for us here, Daddy.

Did you look in that box, Sosha?

Oh, hello there.

Would you like to come home with me?

Oh no, Sosha,
he has a big hole.

Good-bye, Bear.

I wonder how
Bear got that hole.

Do you think anyone will ever want him?

Daddy, maybe that shaggy old bear feels lonely.

We could put tape over the hole . . .

All right, Sosha. Let's go back.

Hurry, Daddy, hurry!

What if he is already gone?

Look.
He's still there.

I would like this bear, please.

Now you will live with me forever,
shaggy old Bear.
I promise.

Bear Is Sick

Welcome home, Bear.

You are not looking well.
And you are leaking.

Let me tape you
closed.

Let's check your
temperature.

Yes, you are very sick.
And you are still leaking.

Let's go to the doctor.

Hello, Doctor. My bear is sick.

Uh-oh! This bear needs stitches.

We're going to make
you better, Bear.

This won't take long.

It's okay, Bear. Be brave.
I'm right here with you.

All done.

No need to worry anymore,
good old Bear.

But you do look weak.
You'd better rest.

Here is some tea, Bear.
It will make you feel better.

Are you bored?
Here is a show for you.

Look at you, Bear.
You're as good as new!

Mister Bear

Sosha! Bear! Time for your bath.

Come on, Bear.
The water feels just
right.

Now, close your eyes!

Let's clean between
the toes.

Isn't this fun, Bear?

Mmm . . .
You smell good.

A good brushing and you'll be so handsome.

Time to get dressed now.

Uh-oh. You don't have any clothes.

Let's see . . .

This is too big!

Too small.

Not your style!

There's nothing right in here.
Let's make something just for you!

How about a jacket, Sosha?
Would you like to pick a color, Bear?

Stop squirming.
We need to measure
you.

Sit still, Bear!
You are so excited.

Here you are, Bear. Your new jacket.

You are all dressed up now.
You look like a gentleman!
I'll have to call you Mister Bear.

Hello, Mister Bear.
How are you, Mister Bear?
I love you, Mister Bear.